Books by Paige Sleuth

Cozy Cat Caper Mystery Series:
Murder in Cherry Hills (Book 1)
Framed in Cherry Hills (Book 2)
Poisoned in Cherry Hills (Book 3)
Vanished in Cherry Hills (Book 4)
Shot in Cherry Hills (Book 5)
Strangled in Cherry Hills (Book 6)
Halloween in Cherry Hills (Book 7)
Stabbed in Cherry Hills (Book 8)
Thanksgiving in Cherry Hills (Book 9)
Frozen in Cherry Hills (Book 10)
Hit & Run in Cherry Hills (Book 11)
Christmas in Cherry Hills (Book 12)
Choked in Cherry Hills (Book 13)
Dropped Dead in Cherry Hills (Book 14)
Valentine's in Cherry Hills (Book 15)
Drowned in Cherry Hills (Book 16)
Orphaned in Cherry Hills (Book 17)
Fatal Fête in Cherry Hills (Book 18)
Arson in Cherry Hills (Book 19)

FATAL FÊTE *in* CHERRY HILLS

COZY CAT

A

CAPER

MYSTERY BOOK

18

PAIGE SLEUTH

CHAPTER ONE

"Kat!" Imogene Little screeched as she flung her front door wide open. "You made it!"

Katherine Harper tucked her brown hair behind her ears and smiled at her friend. "Sorry I'm late. It's Matty's fault. The ornery feline snuck outside as I was leaving, and she absolutely refused to get back in the apartment."

"Can you blame her?" Imogene took a step outside and drew in a long, slow breath, the light of the sun reflecting off of her auburn ponytail. Her hair looked glossier than usual, and she'd traded in her typical jeans and a T-shirt for a pair of black dress slacks and a frilly peach blouse. "It's glorious out here."

Kat had to agree. It was the last Saturday of

March, and the arrival of spring had brought a welcome warm front to Central Washington. It would turn chilly as soon as the sun set, but right now the temperature was perfect.

Imogene stood on her tiptoes to peer over Kat's shoulder. "Where's Andrew?"

"Looking for parking. There's not an empty spot to be found on your block."

"I can't remember a time when I had so many people here. Everybody loves Kenny."

Kat didn't miss how Imogene's face glowed as she said the words, prompting her to wonder how much effort her friend had put into this event. She was fairly certain Imogene wouldn't have bothered with such an elaborate birthday bash if she didn't have a romantic interest in the Cherry Hills police chief. But she didn't want to embarrass her friend by asking.

"How's Clover handling the crowd?" Kat asked. The sheer number of people present today had to be overwhelming for a cat, even one as social as Clover.

"I shut him in my office," Imogene replied, pointing toward the converted den off the dining room. "With people coming in and out, I didn't want to risk him slipping outside unnoticed."

"Smart move."

Imogene grinned. "In all honesty, I believe he was relieved to get away from Frieda. Apparently she has something of an obsession with cats. Before I thought to isolate him, she kept picking him up and carrying him around. It's a wonder he didn't scratch her."

"Who's Frieda?"

"One of Kenny's sisters. She's smitten with Clover. And naturally he wants nothing to do with anybody that interested in him. He barely deigned to let her feed him one of Sam Easton's cream-less tarts."

"Maybe he was holding out for something with real cream in it," Kat suggested.

"Then he has a long wait ahead of him." Imogene motioned Kat inside. "Come and wish Kenny a happy birthday. Andrew can find his own way in when he gets here. Besides, he already got a jump-start on celebrating Kenny's big day. Kenny's officers threw him their own celebration down at the station yesterday."

"I know," Kat said, raising her voice to be heard above the crowd as they moved into the living room. "Andrew saved me a piece of the cake they bought. It was to die for."

"Indeed, it certainly did look divine. Kenny smuggled me a slice too, but unfortunately it wasn't vegan." Imogene stopped near one side of the room. "I still don't think he understands the concept, as many times as I've explained it to him. No meat, no milk, no eggs. How hard is that to comprehend?"

Before Kat could reply, Chief Kenny himself headed toward them. A perplexed furrow marred the burly police chief's brow as he stared at something in his massive hand.

"Imogene, what in the devil is this?" He thrust his arm toward her. "Feels like a sponge —and a dried-up one at that."

"That would be a chickpea pinwheel," Imogene told him.

"Chickpea? Is that anything like a game hen?"

Imogene rolled her eyes. "A chickpea is a garbanzo bean, Kenny."

"Is it edible?"

"Of course."

He pinched the pinwheel between his fingers. "Why is it green?"

"Because there's spinach in the tortilla holding everything together."

Chief Kenny scrunched up his nose.

"Try it," Imogene instructed. "You might like it."

He didn't oblige, choosing instead to pinch the pinwheel between two stubby fingers as though it might bite him. "Fat chance of that. Why you couldn't serve good ol'-fashioned pigs in blankets is beyond me."

"Because I don't support the suffering of animals."

"But it's my birthday."

"Yes, and it's *my* party. As a matter of fact, I distinctly recall you tossing me out of your office when I asked whether you wanted to be involved with the planning."

"I didn't toss you out."

"I believe your exact words were, 'Get out of my office. I have a budget to balance.' "

Chief Kenny scowled. "Well, I didn't reckon you planned to starve us all."

"Starve?" Imogene scoffed. "Every surface in the kitchen is covered with food, thanks to Sam Easton and his catering team. If you don't want the chickpea pinwheel, go get some fried risotto balls."

"What the heck is a risotto?"

"Rice."

Chief Kenny stuck one finger in his mouth in a mock gag.

Imogene flapped her hand. "Fine. Don't eat it if you feel that way. And don't come crying to me next year when you turn fifty-six and nobody is around to celebrate with you."

Kat grinned as the two continued bickering like an old married couple. If they weren't romantically involved yet, she figured it was just a matter of time.

After a minute, the argument started to peter out. And from the smirk on Imogene's face, it was clear she had come out ahead.

"Shoulda known better when you didn't serve a turkey at Thanksgiving," he muttered, stalking off in a sulk.

Imogene made a face at his retreating back before spinning toward Kat. "I should have saved my efforts for somebody more grateful. When is your birthday again?"

"Not till June. And there's no need to throw me a party. I'm not really into birthdays."

"Nonsense! Everybody is into birthdays."

"I'm thirty-two, past the age when they hold any promise."

"Why, you sound just like an old maid!" Imogene tsked. "That dour attitude is more appropriate for someone my age."

"I hope I'm half as youthful as you are when I'm your age." Although Imogene was in her fifties, most days she had more energy than Kat.

A fluffy white ball streaked past them then, knocking Kat against the wall. Next to her, someone screamed and a man spilled his drink.

But the ball didn't slow down, careening around the room like a miniature rocket.

"Clover!" Imogene yelled, sprinting after the cat.

Clover didn't pay her any heed. He veered into the dining area, catching a woman around Kat's age off guard when he darted between her ankles. She yelped and dropped the tray in her hands. It hit the floor with a clatter, sending dozens of bite-sized finger foods rolling in all different directions.

"Oh!" The woman lifted both hands to her mouth.

Clover stopped to see what the commotion was about. Upon spotting the runaway appetizers, he made a quick U-turn and chased after the closest one, batting it into a corner like a soccer player making a goal.

Imogene grabbed the woman's elbow. "Deirdre, are you okay?"

Deirdre peered at her with wide brown eyes. She looked ready to burst into tears. "I dropped the risotto balls. I'm so sorry."

Kat saw now that she wore a white top coupled with black slacks, a classic catering uniform. An apron with the top folded down was cinched at her waist, and her brown hair was pulled back in a bun. Several tendrils hung around the sides of her face.

Imogene patted Deirdre's arm. "Don't worry about it. Sam can whip up more of those in no time."

Deirdre bit her lip. "You don't think he'll be mad?"

"Of course not."

Deirdre didn't look convinced. She pulled at a loose piece of hair, a tear slipping down her cheek.

"I'll explain how the accident couldn't be helped, that my terror of a cat is to blame," Imogene said. A perturbed expression flashed across her face. "How did he escape my office, anyway?"

Another woman jogged into the room, wild brown curls and a loose-fitting floral skirt flouncing around her. "Was that Clover I saw?"

"Frieda!" Imogene folded her arms across her chest. "Did you let Clover out of my office?"

Frieda blinked. "I did not."

Imogene eyed her suspiciously as she scooped up Clover. The feline struggled for a bit, but when it became clear his human wasn't about to release him he draped his head over her arm and stared longingly at the toppled risotto balls.

Frieda spread her palms. "It wasn't me, I

swear." She reached a tentative hand toward Clover. "But since he's out, you won't mind if I pet him, will you?"

Frieda didn't wait for a response before running her hand down Clover's back. The feline whipped his head around, his ears wilting against his head and a meow of protest escaping past his lips when he saw who it was.

"Ohhh, you're so cute I could just eat you up," Frieda cooed, practically rubbing noses with the cat.

Clover's blue eyes widened in alarm. He peered at Imogene and let out a desperate cry for help.

Imogene took a tiny step backward. "I should put him back in the office before he causes any more damage."

Frieda gave Clover's ears a scritch. "Ohhh, you wouldn't do that, would you now, you sweet little angel you?"

A giggle bubbled up Kat's throat. She did her best to keep it from escaping, but she wasn't entirely successful. The demoralized expression on Clover's face was just too much.

Imogene smirked at Kat. "Kat, this is Frieda Tabernathy, Kenny's sister. She traveled all the way from Bellingham to celebrate Kenny's special day."

"I'm *one* of Kenny's sisters," Frieda corrected, straightening away from Clover and extending a hand toward Kat. Her grip was firm, and Kat could see the muscles in her forearm ripple as they shook hands. "Marigold's around here somewhere too. The others couldn't make it."

"How many sisters does Chief Kenny have?" Kat asked.

"Four," Frieda replied. "Or four too many, if you ask him."

Imogene chuckled. "Such a grouch."

"Marigold and I are the youngest. I'm five years younger than Ken, and Mari was born only fourteen months after me." Frieda scanned the living area. "Let me find Mari and you can meet her."

"I'll catch up with you in a minute." Imogene adjusted Clover in her arms. "First I have to get this little hellion squared away."

As though reminded of Clover's presence, Frieda fell right back into her baby-talking persona. "Auntie Frieda will miss you," she crooned, planting a kiss atop Clover's head.

Clover hissed at her through bared teeth. Somehow, Kat didn't think the feline would miss Auntie Frieda nearly as much.

"Oh, there's Marigold," Frieda announced.

"Follow me, Kat."

But they only made it partway through the crowd before a blood-chilling scream echoed through the house. The individual conversations that had been buzzing all around them came to a grinding halt, leaving behind a quiet that felt more deafening than any sound.

Kat froze in her tracks. Turning around, she spotted Imogene standing near the open door of her home office. Clover was nowhere in sight, having apparently escaped his human's grasp.

But the wily cat's disappearance didn't seem to be the cause of Imogene's alarm. Kat watched as Imogene reached for the doorframe, her knees wobbling as if they were on the verge of buckling.

Springing into action, Kat raced over to her friend, her heart pounding harder with every hurried step. It didn't take her long to identify the reason for Imogene's reaction.

In the middle of Imogene's home office, a man lay on the carpet, his limbs akimbo and a blotch of red pooling around his head. The surprised look preserved in his eyes for all of eternity made it infinitely clear they were too late to save him.

CHAPTER TWO

Kat stepped forward to get a better look at the man inside Imogene's office, but Chief Kenny thwarted her progress when he scooted in front of her and slammed the door shut, nearly giving her a broken nose in the process. He spread his arms wide, eyeing the crowd that had started to press closer.

"Back up, everybody," he boomed in that commanding voice of his. "I need all you folks to clear the area."

Kat and Imogene glanced at each other before dutifully retreating a respectable distance away. A soft murmur traveled through the room as each of the guests did the same, everyone breaking off into small groups to trade information and speculation.

"Did you see who was in there?" Kat whispered to Imogene.

"I did," Imogene replied. Thankfully, although her voice still quavered, she no longer seemed to be in danger of collapsing. "It's Landon Tabernathy."

"Tabernathy?" Kat echoed. "Any relation to Chief Kenny's sister?"

"He's Frieda's husband." Imogene shuddered. "*Was* her husband, I suppose I should say."

As though they'd invoked her presence, Frieda Tabernathy herself dashed into view. Her eyes ricocheted from left to right until they landed on Chief Kenny. She rushed over to him, her brown curls resembling an electric force field against the backdrop of her crazed expression.

"Ken, is it true?" she screeched, grabbing his forearm. "Is Landon dead?"

A pained look spread across Chief Kenny's face. "Looks that way, babe. I'm sorry."

Frieda dropped to her knees. The anguished wail that ripped from her throat plunged the rest of the room into silence as everyone abandoned their whispering to gawk at Landon's recent widow.

Chief Kenny crouched down and patted

Frieda's shoulder with one hand. The gesture looked awkward, as though brother and sister weren't used to physical displays of affection. But Frieda was too caught up in her own grief to even acknowledge the police chief's attempt to calm her.

Chief Kenny locked gazes with Imogene, flashing her a pleading look not dissimilar to the one Clover had sported while suffering through the indignity of Frieda's baby talk. Without hesitation, Imogene swooped down to join the huddle, wrapping one arm around Frieda's shoulders as she murmured softly in her ear.

A woman with a sleek brown bob and a saunter that was all hips sidled up to Kat. "What's all the fuss about?"

Kat lifted her chin toward the office door. "A man is dead in there."

"Dead?" The woman's face went pale. She eyed the chickpea pinwheel in her hand as if it might be laced with poison. "From what?"

"I'm not sure." Kat didn't want to mention the pool of blood.

The woman frowned at Frieda. "I take it she found him?"

Frieda was now a sobbing mess despite Imogene's attempts to soothe her. Her face was buried in her hands, but the tears leaked around them nonetheless. Bearing witness to her pain made Kat's chest hurt.

"The man who died was her husband," Kat said.

The woman stumbled backward, the pinwheel slipping through her fingers and landing soundlessly on the carpet. "Landon?" she squeaked. "Landon's dead?"

"Yes." Kat looked at her with a bit more interest. "Did you know him?"

The woman bobbed her head in slow motion, seeming incapable of speech.

"Marigold!" Imogene waved the woman over. "Come help comfort your sister."

Kat regarded the brunette. "You're Frieda's sister?" But of course she was, Kat thought, wondering why she hadn't noticed the resemblance between her and Frieda before. Both women shared the same high cheekbones and hourglass figure.

Marigold crouched down next to Frieda's other side and set her palm on her knee. "Frieda, what can I do?"

Frieda's hands fell away from her face. She blinked at her sister, as though it took her a moment to recognize her. "You can find Landon's killer," she said.

Marigold gasped. "His killer?" She looked at Chief Kenny. "Ken, Landon was *murdered*?"

Chief Kenny shoved his hands in his pockets. "It's up to the medical examiner to determine cause of death."

"Don't go all cop on me, Ken." Marigold stood up and planted her hands on her hips. "Frieda has a right to answers."

"And she'll get them. You'll just have to be patient."

Frieda leaped to her feet and linked elbows with Marigold. Both sisters wore identical expressions of disapproval. Even with tears staining Frieda's cheeks and a combined weight that was still no match for their brother's, the pair looked like a force to be reckoned with. And, judging by the line of sweat popping out on his forehead, Chief Kenny thought so too.

A well-built Hispanic man rushed over to the police chief. "What can I do, Chief?"

Chief Kenny clapped the man on the shoulder, relief washing over his face. He positioned himself to better face the crowd, using the man as a sort of shield as he maneuvered around his sisters and turned his back on their twin glares. "All righty, folks, listen up. This here is Officer Raoul Leon. He's gonna be taking your statements in the kitchen. Individually.

Nobody's allowed to leave the premises until Officer Leon gives you the go-ahead. Got it?"

Raoul straightened, his chest puffing out so much he nearly doubled in size.

"What about Andrew?" Kat asked Chief Kenny. "Why isn't he interviewing us?"

"Detective Milhone will be in charge of supervising the crime scene technicians," Chief Kenny said, his voice loud enough for everyone to hear. "Normally that would be my role, but I'm gonna step aside on this one."

Frieda whipped toward him, causing Marigold, who still had her arm hooked through Frieda's, to almost lose her balance.

"Step aside?" Frieda said, lurching toward the police chief. "Why?"

He squeezed her arm. "I'm too close to this one, babe. With Landon being my brother-in-law, it would be a conflict of interest for me to lead this investigation."

"But you're the most experienced cop here!" Frieda's gaze skirted toward Raoul. She didn't look impressed. "Is anyone else on the Cherry Hills force even qualified to handle a murder?"

Kat stepped forward, prepared to snap out a retort in Andrew's defense, but Chief Kenny spoke before she could.

"Detective Milhone is top notch," he said.

"And Officer Leon here is one of the smartest guys on my force. They'll get to the bottom of this."

Frieda's face turned red as she swiveled her gaze between Chief Kenny and Raoul Leon. If looks could kill, the Cherry Hills Police Department would have just lost two of their finest.

Raoul beckoned Frieda over with a wave of his arm. "Ma'am, if you'll follow me, I'll get this process started."

Frieda scowled at Chief Kenny before trudging after Raoul. The police chief averted his eyes, almost as if he were afraid of his sister.

Kat jolted, that thought leading to another. Was it possible the police chief had removed himself from this case not because of his relationship to the deceased, but because of his relationship to Frieda?

Did Chief Kenny believe his sister had been the one to take her husband's life?

CHAPTER THREE

Raoul seemed to be taking forever to get through the witness interviews. Anxious for her turn, Kat had started timing them. His questioning of one of the caterers was going on twenty minutes now.

"Hey, Kat."

Kat turned to see Sam Easton, the owner of Easton's Eats standing next to her. "Hi, Sam."

He jutted his chin toward the kitchen. "Deirdre still in there?" Although there wasn't a door to the kitchen, Raoul had roped off enough of a buffer zone to prevent curious onlookers from seeing or hearing anything that went on inside.

"Your server? Yes," Kat replied.

He sighed. "Poor girl. I hope he's not giving her the third degree. She wasn't even going to work this event, but Rich fell ill at the last minute."

Kat figured Rich must be one of Sam's employees. "Have you been interviewed yet?" she asked.

"Yeah. I'm just waiting for Deirdre before I take off. I'm her ride." Sam looked around. "Have you seen Imogene anywhere?"

"She went upstairs to lie down." Imogene hadn't looked well after Raoul had finished questioning her. Kat had been itching to ask how things had gone, but her friend had shaken her head before saying she didn't have the strength to talk about it now.

"Huh." Sam dropped his gaze to the piece of paper in his hands, then brought it up for Kat to see. "I was going to give her my invoice, but she probably doesn't want to be bothered."

Kat took the page from him, her eyes hovering over the colorful logo in the top left corner. Under different circumstances, the jaunty fruit basket sporting two grape eyes, a banana smile, and a pineapple hairdo while brandishing a knife and fork in its two stubby raspberry-hands would have made her smile, but the somber atmosphere of the house doused any amusement she might ordinarily find in a silly cartoon.

"Do you need the money now?" she asked.

"Nah. Imogene was going to write me a check after the party ended, but with everything that went down this evening . . ."

"Right." Kat's stomach clenched at the reminder. "I can give this to her later, if you'd like."

"Thanks. I didn't want to leave it lying around."

Deirdre stumbled out of the kitchen then. Her red eyes and puffy face made it clear she'd been crying.

"Deirdre." Sam took a step toward her.

She let out a sob as she collapsed into his arms. "This is so awful."

Sam patted her on the back. "I know. But don't fret over it. The police will catch whoever did this."

"Were you able to help them at all?" Kat asked Deirdre, eager to hear whether the police had unearthed any leads yet.

But Deirdre only shook her head. She tried to smooth out the crumpled tissue in her hand before using it to swipe at her tears. Kat could see her fingers trembling.

Deirdre tilted her head back and gazed up at Sam. "Can we go now?"

"Yes, of course." Sam turned toward Kat. "I

still have some stuff in the kitchen. Could you tell Imogene I'll come back for it later this week?"

Kat nodded. "Sure."

"Thanks, Kat." He offered her a lopsided smile before wrapping an arm around Deirdre's shoulders and guiding her through the crowd that had been slowly dwindling as Raoul concluded his interviews. He looked relieved to finally be out of there.

Kat knew exactly how he felt. She checked the time on her cell phone and sighed. How long was it going to be before Raoul called her in, anyway? Andrew's interviews never took this long.

Of course, Andrew was a more experienced detective, Kat reminded herself. Perhaps Raoul was still getting a feel for the process. She would just have to be patient.

Raoul poked his head out of the kitchen. His eyes homed in on her, and he summoned her with a crooked forefinger. "Come with me, please."

Kat exhaled, nearly tripping over her feet in her haste. "Finally."

His eyes narrowed.

"I mean, yes, Officer Leon, I'm on my way," Kat amended, forcing herself not to look too keen to get this over with.

It didn't take long for Kat to see why the interviews were taking so long. Raoul seemed to think being a good detective meant asking so many questions that eventually a person couldn't help but trip up over something. After instructing her to walk through every little thing she'd done since stepping through Imogene's front door, he posed a series of questions that merely rehashed what she'd already told him. The whole process left her itching to tear her own hair out.

"Let me get this straight," Raoul said thirty, excruciating minutes into their session. "You had never met Landon Tabernathy before this evening?"

"No," Kat replied curtly, silently adding, *For the fifth time, no.*

"Hmm." Raoul paced from the refrigerator to the sink and back again, pausing to shoot her a sidelong glance every third step.

Kat squelched an eye roll. "What about you?" she asked. "Did you know him?"

He came to an abrupt halt and squared his shoulders. "I'm the one doing the questioning here."

Kat's patience snapped. "You've made that quite clear by rephrasing the same five questions a million different ways. But that doesn't change the fact that I don't have any answers."

Raoul regarded her for a moment that stretched into one minute, then two. She met his assessing gaze with one of her own. She'd had enough, and she wasn't going to let him intimidate her into feeling less worthy for not having any useful information to share. She couldn't help what she'd seen—or not seen—and she refused to feel guilty about it.

Finally, he gave a slight nod and tucked his notebook in his breast pocket. "All right then," he said. "In that case, we're done here. But I want to be the first person you call if you remember anything later." He yanked a business card out of his breast pocket and snapped it between his fingers before holding it out to her.

She took it. "Of course." With great restraint, she managed not to break into a run as she hurried across the kitchen.

"Wait!"

Raoul's shout halted her in her tracks.

"One final word before I let you go," he said.

"What's that?"

"Stay out of this."

She frowned. "What?"

Raoul leaned against the counter, but he didn't look the least bit relaxed. "I know you have a reputation around town for attracting crime. Wherever you go, trouble seems to follow."

Kat bristled. "That's hardly my fault."

"Either way, you need to leave the investigating to the police."

"I plan to." Then, simply because she couldn't resist the barb, she added, "I have complete faith in Detective Milhone's ability to get to the bottom of this."

Raoul's eyes darkened.

"He's the most competent policeman I've ever met," she went on. She wasn't sure why she was so intent on needling Raoul. Evidently she was more sensitive than she'd thought to insinuations that she might have had something to do with the previous crimes she'd found herself involved in.

"That he is," Raoul said, his voice clipped. "But just because the two of you are swapping spit, don't think that gives you a pass to butt into police business."

Kat's face reddened. "You're way—"

"My original point remains," Raoul barked, cutting her off. "You should trust me—the police —to handle this investigation. In that spirit, I expect this will be our last time chatting about Mr. Tabernathy's passing." He regarded her down the length of his nose. "Unless, of course, you're guilty."

Kat gritted her teeth, but she didn't say anything, telling herself that he was merely doing his job.

After all, she might not be guilty, but someone at this party sure was.

CHAPTER FOUR

"Thank you for inviting me over," Imogene said, bursting through Kat's front door.

"No problem." Although, Kat hadn't extended an invitation so much as Imogene had wheedled one out of her. Imogene had phoned her not three minutes after she'd left the party, lamenting over how her home was now a crime scene and how the taint of a murder had rendered her incapable of drawing air into her lungs, leaving her in danger of suffocating if she didn't get out of there soon. After that, how could Kat not offer up her home as a temporary refuge?

Imogene slumped onto one sofa. Matty, Kat's tortoiseshell, crooked one eye at their visitor, a silent reprimand for Imogene's failure to seat herself delicately upon the couch that Matty thought of as her own. But Matty wasn't one to hold a grudge. Before long, the yellow-and-brown feline allowed her eyelids to droop closed once again.

"I asked Raoul when he expects to leave, and he said he intended to stay for as long as it takes." Imogene huffed. "As long as it takes! What does he plan to do, move into my guest room?"

"I'm sure he's anxious to nab Landon's killer," Kat said, doing her best to see things from Raoul Leon's angle, even if he had rubbed her the wrong way during her interview.

Imogene crossed her legs. "Yes, well, I just can't bear the thought of slipping into my pj's when he's mucking around downstairs looking for detritus a murderer might have left behind."

"What does he think he might find?"

Imogene threw her hands up, the sudden gesture causing Matty to startle. "Who knows?"

Matty's nose twitched in disapproval before she stretched her front legs out and settled back down.

Imogene scooted closer to Matty and rested her hand on the cat's back. "I just can't abide the notion of a murderer leaving things in my house. Can you imagine the nerve?"

"Raoul might have been referring to DNA or something microscopic," Kat pointed out, sitting down on the opposite sofa.

Imogene traced her finger along the pattern in Matty's fur. "I suppose that's true." She straightened. "But still! How am I ever going to relax in my own home again?"

The faint sounds of a cat scratching in litter became evident in the silence that fell then. Since Matty was out here, Kat knew the culprit had to be Tom.

No sooner had that thought entered her mind when the black-and-brown cat in question came tearing down the hallway as swiftly as if he'd unearthed a mouse while rearranging the contents of the litter pan. He zoomed straight toward the cat tree by the window, a few stray pieces of litter landing on Kat's feet as he kicked up his paws. Upon reaching his destination, he clawed at one of the sisal posts before spinning around with a crazed look in his eyes and bounding off into the kitchen.

Kat grinned. It wasn't unusual for Tom to act out after a trip to the bathroom. Apparently covering up one's business had some invigorating properties not found when flushing an ordinary toilet.

Imogene watched the cat without so much as a smile, clearly preoccupied by other matters. "I'll tell you," she said, "if Kenny were the one investigating Landon's murder, he would have been out of my house by now."

"You can't expect Raoul to work as fast as Chief Kenny or Andrew. He's used to writing traffic tickets, not hunting down murderers."

"Hrrmph." Imogene looked at Matty as if the feline might offer her the support she had expected to receive from Kat. "I don't like that Kenny isn't taking the lead on this."

"He doesn't want there to be any sense of impropriety, given his conflict of interest."

Imogene flicked her wrist. "Disliking Landon wouldn't stop Kenny from throwing his heart and soul into that investigation."

Kat perked up. "Chief Kenny didn't like Landon?" This was the first time she'd heard of any friction between the two.

Imogene flushed, but she was spared from responding immediately when Tom came running back into the room. Upon spotting Imogene, his green eyes lit up and he meowed his way over to her. Imogene reached down to pet him, but she moved with a stiffness that betrayed her discomfort.

"What was Chief Kenny's beef with Landon?" Kat pressed, unwilling to let Imogene off the hook so easily.

"Oh, nothing unusual." Imogene kept her eyes trained on Tom. "He simply never warmed to him."

"Huh." Kat had to wonder just how much the police chief had disliked his brother-in-law. Enough to commit murder?

Imogene brought her gaze up to meet Kat's. "You're not thinking Kenny had anything to do with Landon's death, are you?"

Imogene's tone made it clear the question was one of Kat's loyalties more than anything else. "I sure hope not," Kat replied carefully.

Imogene scowled. "If you ask me, Raoul has more to gain from killing Landon than Kenny."

Kat blinked, unsure if she'd heard right. "Raoul Leon knew Landon Tabernathy?" If that were true, she had to wonder if Chief Kenny knew about their connection. She didn't figure the police chief would have put the officer on the case if he did.

"No," Imogene said, doing her best to stroke Tom while he twined between her ankles, "but did you see how excited he was when Kenny put him in charge of questioning everybody? He looked like he'd hit the lotto."

"He was probably happy to be tasked with

something more intellectually stimulating than monitoring speed traps."

"Exactly." Imogene looked triumphant as she gave Tom one last vigorous scratch between the ears before settling back against the couch. "Landon's murder gives Raoul a chance to prove himself. He had to have known Kenny would remove himself from any investigation involving one of his own kin, even if they were only related by marriage. That means he'd either have to bring Raoul in to help or let Andrew flounder on his own."

Kat's jaw clenched. "I doubt Andrew would have floundered."

Imogene either didn't catch the bite in Kat's tone or chose to ignore it. "It's no secret Raoul wants to move up the ranks. And what better way to prove he's worthy of a promotion than to solve a murder?"

With Imogene no longer paying him any attention, Tom ambled over to Kat and jumped into her lap. She petted him as she considered Imogene's words. Could there be some truth to what she was saying? Raoul had been awfully heavy-handed during her witness interview. And everyone at the Cherry Hills Police Department knew he was ambitious. Andrew had told her in the past that Raoul's lack of a promotion so far had been more the result of a shortage of positions rather than because he wasn't qualified. Maybe he figured if he could do a good job with the investigation into Landon's death, Chief Kenny would have no choice but to make him a detective.

"Of course," Imogene said, "if Raoul wants to use this whole thing to showcase his detective skills, he has to actually find Landon's killer."

A chill worked its way down Kat's spine. Imogene was right. Raoul wouldn't impress anyone if Landon's murder went unsolved or he concluded things with his own guilty confession. That meant if he *had* orchestrated Landon's death to give his career a boost, he fully intended to frame someone—someone innocent.

And, given his comments in the kitchen, Kat feared the someone he had in his sights might very well be her.

CHAPTER FIVE

Sunday morning, Kat wanted nothing more than to sleep in. Imogene hadn't returned home until well after midnight, leaving Kat to stew over whether Raoul Leon could possibly be involved with the very murder he had been tasked to solve. One minute she would be convinced Raoul was guilty, and the next she was positive Imogene had only suggested as much to deflect suspicion off Chief Kenny and his family. The internal conflict kept her up until close to dawn.

But Kat's restless night was of no concern to Matty. The tortoiseshell jumped on the bed promptly at six, not about to delay breakfast for anyone.

Matty had developed a system for rousing

her human in the nine months since Kat had adopted her. She always started off with a simple meow delivered as she sat perched atop the nightstand. Although Matty wasn't nearly as vocal as Tom, she wasn't above voicing herself if that was what it took for food to appear in the kitchen.

If the meow didn't prove sufficient, Matty would move on to more extreme tactics. Those ranged from leaning in close to Kat's ear while purring at top volume, to patting Kat lightly on the face, to sitting on Kat's chest. Typically Kat would relent after a few minutes, knowing Matty wouldn't give up until she got her way.

But this morning Kat felt much more sluggish than normal. As much as she tried to force her legs into gear, they refused to cooperate. If she could get just five more minutes of sleep . . .

Matty, who had been stomping up and down Kat's torso for the past two minutes, stopped pacing. She seemed to be at a loss as to what to try next. Even with her eyes closed, Kat could picture the bewildered look on the tortoiseshell's face, unable to remember a time when the feline had been required to escalate her antics past this point.

But as it happened, Matty wasn't the one who finally forced Kat out of bed. Usually content to let his sister act as the alarm clock, Tom had evidently reached his limit. Still lying on Kat's pillow where he took to sleeping most nights, he whacked Kat in the face with his tail and howled directly into her right ear.

Kat bolted upright, sending Matty scrambling for solid ground. "All right!" she said, throwing the covers aside. "I get the message."

The felines exchanged triumphant looks before following her to the kitchen.

After the animals were fed, Kat changed into jeans and a lightweight sweater and drove over to Jessie's Diner for her own breakfast. The Sunday morning rush was in full swing when she stepped through the restaurant's front door. The buzz of conversation filled her ears as the heavenly scent of hash browns, bacon, and pancakes flooded her nose. Her mouth was watering before she even slipped into one of the last few empty booths in the dining area.

She perused the specials board while she waited for her server, debating between the apple pancakes and a plain old mushroom omelet. She pictured Imogene bustling around her kitchen at home, and she wondered whether Raoul Leon was still hanging around, forcing Imogene to step around him in order to cook her own breakfast.

". . . murdered Landon," a male voice said.

Kat felt as if she'd been struck by a bolt of lightning. She jerked in her seat, peering around in an attempt to identify the speaker.

"Marigold wouldn't have killed him." This time, the voice belonged to a woman. "She loved him."

"In high school," the man amended. "That was a long time ago."

The exchange was taking place behind her, Kat realized. She lifted up her spoon, rotating it around until she caught the reflection of the couple seated at the next booth over. A middle-aged man sat facing her, his fleshy jowls looking disproportionately huge in the spoon's curved metal surface. She couldn't see the woman's face, only the mass of brown hair that hung past her shoulders.

But Kat didn't have to see the woman's face to know who she was. Belinda and Colin Bridges were Jessie's Diner regulars. She had often served the couple when she was still waitressing here.

"It doesn't matter how much time has passed," Belinda said. "Nobody forgets their first love."

"Precisely what I've been trying to tell you," Colin replied. "Marigold undoubtedly remembers how this Landon chap broke her heart way back when. And the fact that he gave her the boot to marry her sister would be a definite blow to the ego."

"You don't know what you're talking about. If she were that torn up about it, she would have offed him a long time ago."

"This could've been her first opportunity."

"Are you kidding me? He's married to her sister. She must have seen him countless times over the years."

In the spoon's reflection, Kat observed Colin resettling in his seat. "Seen, yes," he said. "Gotten alone? Most likely not. Landon lived in Bellingham, remember, and last I heard Marigold was calling Portland home."

Belinda flopped back in her own seat with enough force for a runaway lock of her hair to brush Kat's neck on the other side of the booth seat. The next thing Kat knew, Belinda's wide green eyes were looming in the spoon's face.

"Kat!"

The spoon tumbled out of Kat's hand, landing noisily on the floor. "Oh, hi, Belinda."

"Look at you sitting there just like a regular customer!"

"I am a customer," Kat said, smiling. "I no longer work here, remember?"

"Naturally, I know that. I may be considered a senior according to Jessie's menu, but my memory hasn't deserted me yet." Belinda scrutinized her. "Have you been sitting there eavesdropping this whole time?"

Kat flushed. "I'm sorry. I didn't mean to—"

"Well, of course you did," Belinda said, but the way her lips twitched suggested she was more amused than angry. "You are the town detective, after all."

"I think you're confusing me with Andrew."

Belinda flapped her hand. "We know he's the official Cherry Hills police detective. But you're quite the investigator in your own right. Don't deny it."

"She's right," Colin piped up, a grin rearranging his jowls. "You have quite a reputation in Cherry Hills."

Kat couldn't think of anything to say. After all, she *had* found herself caught up in more than her share of crimes since she'd returned to town last summer.

Colin wobbled back and forth as though he were getting comfortable in his seat. "So, tell us your opinion of this Landon Tabernathy business."

"I don't really have an opinion," Kat said.

"That's why she was eavesdropping on us,"

Belinda told Colin. "She's still sizing up the players."

"I wasn't really eavesdropping." The words popped out of Kat's mouth automatically—and needlessly, she couldn't help thinking. The smirk on Belinda's face indicated she wasn't buying it.

Belinda twisted sideways to face Kat better. "Colin and I were just discussing what a playboy Landon was back in the day."

"We knew him when he lived in Cherry Hills," Colin replied.

"This would have been in high school," Belinda added.

"Before he and Frieda got hitched at the end of senior year. That would have been, when? 1983?"

"No, we graduated in '85, and they were only a year ahead of us."

Colin tapped his chin. "So, 1984 then. Thirty-two years ago now."

"Hard to believe, isn't it?" Belinda turned toward Kat. "Back then Landon was dating Marigold."

Colin shook his head. "He wasn't dating her. She had taken a shine to him, but Landon did not share her sentiments."

"Well, if he wasn't dating her he was certainly leading her on," Belinda replied.

"He led all the girls on. I wouldn't be surprised if he slept with half the school."

Belinda faced Kat. "I was part of the other half, mind you. I only had eyes for Colin."

Colin beat a fist against his chest. "I was more muscle than padding back then."

Kat smiled politely but refrained from commenting. It was clear the Bridges thought her presence here was extraneous, and she was perfectly content to sit back and listen to them talk.

"Landon wasn't too bad-looking himself," Belinda said. "It was no wonder all the girls fawned over him."

"He'd probably still be playing the field, if Frieda hadn't convinced him to marry her."

Belinda shook her head. "*She* didn't convince him. It was that father of hers." She peered at Kat again. "Her father had that linebacker's build, just like Kenny. He didn't like the idea of a daughter of his running around with a man without making things official."

"Kenny wasn't too keen on them getting hitched, if I remember correctly," Colin said.

"No, he wasn't," Belinda agreed. "He didn't figure marriage would change Landon's penchant for sleeping around. I heard from

Marigold that their differing opinions resulted in quite a few arguments between him and his father."

"Of course, ultimately it was Frieda's decision," Colin said.

"And she chose to marry Landon despite Kenny's objections."

Colin tapped one finger against the tabletop. "I heard he was hot and heavy with another girl before he agreed to marry Frieda."

"Yes, Marigold," Belinda told him.

"No, not Marigold. That Solomon girl."

"Rita?" Belinda looked pensive. "You're right. I forgot they were something of an item before her family moved away."

"They were no more of an item than Landon and his other conquests."

"What ever happened to her?"

"She's living in Wenatchee now," Colin said. "Martin spotted her on a trip up there to buy ties. She rang up his purchases."

"That doesn't sound right." Belinda pursed her lips. "Is he sure it was her?"

Colin shrugged. "That's what he said."

"I thought she was going to be a doctor."

"Perhaps she couldn't handle the school-work."

"That's rubbish. She was the best student in

the entire class of '84!"

"That was before she met Landon." Colin waggled his eyebrows. "He no doubt opened her eyes to the fact that there was more to the world than textbooks." He grabbed Belinda's hand. "Just like how I opened up your eyes."

Belinda slipped her hand out of his grasp and swatted his knuckles. "Oh, go on now."

"It's true." Colin looked at Kat. "Not that I played the field like Landon. I was besotted with Belinda from the start. No other girl could ever turn my head."

Belinda squinted at him. "I don't believe they tried."

"How quickly you forget. Kat, I'll have you know, I was quite the stud back in my younger years." He flexed one bicep. "I still have it, to an extent."

Belinda giggled. "The only thing you have is an overinflated ego. Don't you agree, Kat?"

Kat didn't reply. Her head was spinning. She was used to having Belinda and Colin tag-team her when ordering a meal, but never when it came to furnishing information potentially relevant to a homicide. She couldn't help thinking that breakfast orders were a bit easier to follow—and the consequences not nearly as dire if she happened to get something wrong.

"Anyhoo," Belinda said, "our point is that Landon wasn't shy about bedding as many high school girls as he could. But his reputation wasn't a secret. Anyone who got involved with him had to know he was just in it for the fun."

"You're assuming women think rationally," Colin countered. "Why, I wouldn't be surprised if one of Landon's conquests popped up at Imogene's party to exact revenge for some perceived slight she'd suffered when he didn't limit his attentions to her all those years ago."

Belinda flicked her wrist. "Poppycock. Nobody would have nurtured a grudge for that long."

"You've held grudges for longer when I've left the toilet seat up."

"With good reason. How hard is it to put the seat down?"

"Precisely. Wouldn't it be easier to put it down yourself than to nag me about putting it down?"

"That's not the point. The point is . . ."

Kat tuned out when it became clear the toilet-seat argument might go on for a while. Instead, she tried to sort through everything the Bridges had told her about Landon.

Could Colin be right? Could someone from Landon's past have killed him? Just how angry had Marigold been when her high school crush chose her sister over her?

Enough to still want to punish him all these years later?

CHAPTER SIX

Kat was still mulling over the information Belinda and Colin Bridges had thrown at her when she left Jessie's Diner. The two had argued on more points than they'd agreed, their individual recollections of their high school days so out of alignment that Kat found it hard to give much merit to anything either one of them said. It was impossible to determine which one had the more accurate memory.

A slight headache had begun to throb on the left side of her head by the time she parked in the lot outside her apartment building and headed for the front entrance. At least Belinda and Colin had agreed on one thing: Landon Tabernathy had been a young Lothario. But Kat was at a loss as to whether that had factored into his death.

"Hey!"

Kat paused mid-step. Was that one of Chief Kenny's sisters waving at her?

"Thank goodness you're back," Marigold said, clasping her hands in front of her. "I didn't know how long you'd be, but now I'm glad I waited."

Kat was sure to stand a few feet away from her unexpected visitor. Marigold's sudden presence outside her home left her unsettled, especially in light of everything Belinda and Colin had shared over breakfast.

Marigold frowned, as though she had expected a warmer welcome. "You are Kat Harper, right?"

"I am," Kat confirmed, figuring there was no point in denying it.

"Maybe you don't remember me. I'm Marigold, Kenny's youngest sister. We met at his birthday party yesterday. Although, I missed your name at the time."

"I remember." Kat hugged her purse closer. "Is there something I can help you with?"

Marigold's face brightened. "Why, yes. You can help me find Landon's killer."

Kat's jaw slipped open. "Why are you asking me? Your brother is the chief of police."

"It was his idea I come to you. Kenny says you're like a private investigator of sorts. He gave me your address. And since he has a 'conflict of interest' "—Marigold made air quotes as if the conflict only existed in Chief Kenny's imagination—"I thought maybe you could do a little digging."

"Or you could leave the investigating to the two, very qualified members of the Cherry Hills Police Department assigned to the case," Kat said, pushing aside her doubts about Raoul Leon.

"With Landon being Frieda's husband, she's going to be their main suspect. I can't just sit by and do nothing while they build a case against her." Marigold chewed on her bottom lip. "But I don't know the first thing about solving a murder. That's why I thought maybe you could help get to the bottom of things."

Kat studied her. She did look sincere. And while the long-term residents of Cherry Hills might have some insight into Landon's high school days, if they were anything like the Bridges they likely hadn't spoken to him in thirty-two years. Marigold, on the other hand, was his sister-in-law. It stood to reason she'd seen Landon more than a few times in the past three decades.

"Do the police have a cause of death yet?" Kat asked.

Marigold wrapped her arms around her middle. "I heard he might have received a blow to the head."

"Like somebody punched him?" Marigold wasn't very large. Would she be capable of punching a man with enough force to kill him?

"Or he was struck with something," Marigold said.

"With what?"

Marigold lifted one shoulder. "Nobody knows, and Ken says the medical examiner might not get to Landon's autopsy until later today."

Although Chief Kenny had formally removed himself from the case, he evidently was keeping up to speed with new developments. Kat couldn't blame him. She was curious herself, and she hadn't even known Landon. It didn't escape her awareness that by agreeing to work with Marigold she would have access to the same information as the police.

Her mind made up, Kat pointed to the door. "Would you like to come inside?"

Marigold bobbed her head. "Yes. Yes, I would like that very much."

They didn't speak on the way up to Kat's

third-floor unit. Kat still wasn't sure whether she could trust Marigold, and Marigold looked a bit wary herself, as if she were having second thoughts about accompanying a stranger to her apartment.

Tom met them at the door, exhibiting none of the same caution as he meowed frantically and weaved around Marigold's ankles. His un-abashed enthusiasm would have put Kat more at ease had the friendly feline not been known to have solicited attention from criminals before.

"Hi there, kitty," Marigold crooned as she crouched down to stroke Tom. "You're a chatty one, aren't you?"

"Tom is as social as cats come," Kat told her, closing the front door and tossing her purse on the coffee table. She pointed to the couch where Matty was curled up, one eye pried open to observe the activity. "His sister, on the other hand, will make you work for her affections."

"At least she's not running away."

"That would mean admitting you matter. Matty would never do anything to make herself appear less superior to a human."

Tom, however, had no qualms about beg-ging for pats. He stood on his hind feet and dragged one cheek against Marigold's fingers. She responded by giving him a vigorous full-body rub that made him purr in approval.

Kat perched on one of the couch armrests, deciding to get down to business. "I have to say, I'm surprised you're so interested in clearing your sister's name."

Marigold glanced at her. "Why's that?"

"I got the impression you and your sister weren't all that close."

Marigold swayed back a little, Tom temporarily forgotten. "Why would you think that?"

"I heard she stole Landon from you."

Marigold sighed. "He was never really mine."

"But you liked him."

"I guess. But that was years ago. I wouldn't kill him because he chose Frieda." Marigold smiled ruefully. "Frankly, he made the right decision. Frieda's always been more stable than me."

"More stable?" Kat echoed.

"A homemaker type. I was the one who liked to sneak out to parties and whatnot, while Frieda stayed home and worked on her school assignments."

"Even so, you must have been upset when she went after Landon."

Marigold pressed her lips together. She took a long moment, as though considering how to respond.

"Okay," she finally said, "I admit I wasn't happy when Frieda started dating Landon. She knew I liked him, and it's kind of an unspoken rule that you don't go after your sister's crush. But she didn't, really."

"Didn't what?" Kat asked.

"Pursue Landon. *He* was the one who went after her."

"She could have turned him down."

"I don't know about that. Landon had this charm about him. He was hard to resist. I couldn't really blame her when she agreed to go out with him, and then later when she fell in love."

"No matter how charming Landon was, you must have blamed Frieda somewhat," Kat said.

"Well, sure," Marigold replied. "I was mad at her, but I wouldn't have killed anyone over it. And, if I *were* angry enough to commit murder, I certainly wouldn't have waited until now to do it."

"Are you married?" Kat hadn't noticed a ring on her finger.

"No, I never found the right guy."

"Or you never found anyone who stacked up

to Landon," Kat proposed.

Marigold barked out a laugh. "I'm not still pining over him, if that's what you're thinking. And if I was, why would I kill him?"

"Because you couldn't have him."

"I didn't want him," Marigold insisted. "He was merely the object of a teenage infatuation, one I got over thirty years ago."

"Then maybe you killed him to punish Frieda for stealing him away."

"I would never do that."

Kat regarded Marigold as she tried to gauge her sincerity. She had to give Marigold credit for maintaining eye contact. Would a guilty person be capable of that? Maybe, if they didn't regret what they'd done.

Marigold blew out a breath. "Look. Frieda and I might have done some hurtful things over the years, but we'd never go so far as that. No matter how mad we might be, we would defend each other to the death." She grimaced. "That was a bad choice of words. But you know what I mean. We've got each other's backs no matter what."

Kat fingered the edge of the couch. Not having any siblings of her own, she found the dynamics between them fascinating and mysterious. What would it be like to share that kind of bond with someone?

For that matter, could such a fierce sense of loyalty drive one sibling to kill on another's behalf? Maybe Marigold hadn't killed Landon for revenge so much as a favor to Frieda. Did Frieda have a reason to want him dead?

Marigold lowered herself onto the sofa across from Kat. "I'm telling you the truth. I didn't kill Landon."

"Why should I believe you?" Kat asked.

"Because I'm here, aren't I? I'm asking you to investigate. Would I do that if I were guilty?"

"You might if Chief Kenny put you up to it."

Marigold worked her jaw for a second. "What about Frieda? You can't possibly think she's guilty."

"I don't know her well enough to have an opinion one way or another."

Marigold nodded slowly. "Fair enough. Are you at least open to considering other suspects besides my sister and me?"

"I am," Kat conceded.

"Then there's just one thing to do," Marigold announced as she jumped off the couch. Her sudden movement startled Tom into a fighting position, his back arched and his tail expanded to three times its normal size.

"What's that?" Kat asked.

"Go talk to Frieda and find out who had it in for Landon."

CHAPTER SEVEN

It was impossible for Kat and Marigold to say much during the drive to the Cherry Hills Hotel. Tom's distressed protests from the back seat had grown steadily louder with each passing minute. Kat had to remind herself that Tom wasn't actually being tortured, despite how his nonstop yowling might indicate otherwise. He was only acting out in response to a hatred of being confined in a cat carrier, and an even more intense hatred of car rides.

When the feline paused for air, Kat shot a glance at Marigold in the passenger seat. "Why did we have to bring Tom again?"

"Because Frieda won't open the door otherwise," Marigold replied, examining her nails. "Trust me. I sat outside her hotel room for two hours yesterday, begging her to let me in. And you know what she did? She refused! Me, her very own sister who was only trying to be there in her time of need. But she loves cats." Marigold reached into the back seat and tapped on the carrier door. "She won't be able to resist you, big guy."

The excuse sounded flimsy in Kat's opinion, but she figured there was no point in arguing. After all, they were almost at the hotel. It made no sense to turn around now.

Fortunately, the Cherry Hills Hotel welcomed pets, saving Kat from the hassle of figuring out how to sneak a caterwauling feline inside. Judging by the alarmed looks Tom garnered from the desk clerk and the couple currently checking in as he wailed his way through the lobby, Kat didn't figure they ever would have made it past the automatic doors otherwise.

"She's in room one-thirteen," Marigold said, leading the way.

Kat inspected the room numbers as they moved down the hallway. "Here," she said.

Marigold rapped on the door three times. "Frieda? It's me."

There was a pause before Frieda shouted back, "I told you, I don't want to see you right now."

Marigold leaned closer to the door. "Kat Harper is here, too. And she brought you her therapy cat, to help with your grief."

Kat frowned. "Well, he's not exactly a *thera —*"

"Shh," Marigold hissed, pinching her arm.

A slight commotion could be heard behind the door. "Who did you say is with you?" Frieda asked, her voice sounding much closer now.

"Kat Harper, the PI Kenny told me about," Marigold replied.

"I'm not a—" Kat began.

Marigold pinched her arm again. "She's here with her therapy cat, Tom."

At the mention of his name, Tom meowed at the top of his lungs.

"That's Tom," Marigold announced. "Hear how anxious he is to meet you? He's trained to recognize when people are in distress."

Kat fidgeted, uncomfortable going along with this charade. But Marigold clearly didn't share Kat's qualms. She gave Kat a conspiratorial wink as if they were merely playing a game.

"Oh, all right." Frieda's grudging capitulation was punctuated by the scrape of a deadbolt turning.

Marigold flashed Kat a triumphant smile

that stretched across most of her face and crinkled the skin around her eyes. In that one brief instant, Kat could clearly see the resemblance between her and Chief Kenny.

Frieda, on the other hand, looked as though she might never smile again. She swung the door open with a scowl planted firmly on her face. Her eyes brightened briefly when they landed on Tom, but darkened just as quickly when her gaze reached Marigold.

"I'm here," she said, her voice tight. "What do you want?"

Marigold's lower lip jutted out. "Is that any way to greet your sister?"

"When the sister is you, yes."

"Hey, I'm here to help you."

Without waiting for a response, Marigold pushed past Frieda. She stood in the middle of the hotel room and lifted her chin in defiance.

Frieda exhaled forcibly enough to rearrange the curls on her forehead. "You might as well come in too, Kat."

Kat obeyed, surveying her surroundings as she entered. The sight of a man's shaving kit on the bathroom counter drew her up short. Knowing the owner of that kit was now dead sent a chill through her bones.

The door clicked shut, and Frieda stepped

past Kat. She stood a few feet away from Marigold, both of them glaring at each other. Kat hovered by the door, unsure of what to do. Frieda obviously didn't want them here, but she was also the most qualified person to answer any questions about Landon.

Tom broke the tension when he meowed. He poked one brown-and-black-striped paw between the carrier slats, reaching toward Frieda.

Frieda's face softened, and she touched the tip of her index finger to Tom's paw. "Hey there, beautiful." Then she narrowed her eyes at Marigold. "Are you sure he's allowed in here?"

"This is a pet-friendly establishment," Kat assured her.

"Then there's no reason to keep him confined to a cage." Frieda shut the bathroom door. "Go ahead and let him out."

Kat moved farther into the room and set the carrier on the floor. Tom came slinking out as soon as she released the door latch. He rubbed his face against Kat's sneaker before sniffing at his new surroundings.

Frieda sat on the edge of one of the room's two queen-size beds and watched him. After a moment, she asked, "What exactly makes him a therapy cat?"

Kat smiled sheepishly. "He's not really."

Frieda scowled at Marigold. Evidently she was used to being duped by her younger sister. It made Kat wonder whether lying was second nature to Marigold. Had she fooled Kat earlier too, when she'd claimed not to have anything to do with Landon's death?

"Kat here has agreed to catch Landon's killer," Marigold said.

"I agreed to help," Kat clarified.

Frieda cocked her head. "How long have you been a PI?"

"I'm not. I work in an office."

Marigold let out a shrill laugh and swatted Kat on the shoulder. "You're so modest."

Kat took a step away from her. "I'm not modest, and I'm not a PI." She was no longer willing to continue misleading Frieda now that she'd let them inside. "I've just happened to help solve a few recent crimes."

"And now she's going to solve Landon's murder!" Marigold chirped.

Frieda's lips puckered. She didn't look convinced. Kat couldn't blame her. In Frieda's eyes she had just gone from a private investigator with a trained therapy animal to a common office drudge who happened to own an unremarkable house cat.

Marigold pulled out the chair tucked under

the desk bolted to one wall and sat down. "So, Kat, about who might have killed Landon . . ."

Frieda hadn't kicked her out yet, so Kat figured she might as well ask her questions. "Frieda, I was curious whether Landon had any enemies that you know of."

Frieda frowned. "Enemies?"

"Anyone who might have wanted to see him . . . gone."

Frieda sat up. "No, of course not."

"You're sure?"

"Well, no. But why would Ken invite Landon's enemies to his birthday party?"

"I understand Landon grew up here."

"Yeah." Frieda made a gesture that encompassed Marigold. "We all did."

"Landon was a player," Marigold blurted out.

"Mari!" Frieda scolded.

"What?" Marigold tilted her chin up. "It's true."

Kat twisted toward Frieda. "Is it true?" She had gathered as much from Belinda and Colin Bridges—at least, if Landon hadn't changed his ways in the past three decades—but she wanted to hear it from Frieda directly.

Frieda's face flamed. "I suppose there might be a teensy bit of truth to that."

"A teensy bit?" Marigold scoffed. "Try a huge, whopping truckload of truth."

"All right." Frieda tossed her hands in the air. "So Landon liked to flirt a little. So what? He still didn't deserve to die."

"No," Kat said slowly, "but his behavior might have made the wrong person jealous."

"You're talking about me." Frieda's tone was like ice.

Kat shrugged.

Frieda glared at her sister. "Is this why you came over here? To accuse me of murdering my husband?"

"Just the opposite," Marigold said. "We're trying to dig up more suspects. And if you don't like our questions, you have nobody to blame but yourself. You asked me to help find Landon's killer, remember? How are we supposed to do that without asking questions?"

Frieda didn't say anything, continuing to shoot daggers at her sister. Oblivious to the mounting tension, Tom jumped onto the bed and nudged Frieda's elbow with his head. When that wasn't enough to get her attention, he meowed.

Frieda's face transformed as she shifted her gaze to the cat. She cradled Tom's head in her hands and made kissing noises at him. Tom rewarded her by revving up his purring and snuggling into her lap.

Kat watched him in awe. Maybe he *would* make a good therapy cat.

"So, Kat," Marigold said, "you think Landon's womanizing is what got him killed?"

"I don't know," Kat replied. "But so far it's the only questionable thing about his lifestyle that's come to light."

"You can't deny he liked to turn on the charm." Marigold looked at Frieda when she said the words, as though waiting for her sister to concur.

But Frieda didn't meet her eye. Instead, she concentrated on petting Tom.

"Did you notice him flirting with anybody at the party?" Kat asked Marigold.

Marigold huffed. "A better question would be whether I noticed anyone he *didn't* flirt with."

"Hey." Frieda raised her head. "That's not fair."

"Is it really?" Marigold challenged.

Frieda clamped her mouth shut, then pried it open to say, "He only hit on women."

Marigold snorted. "Okay, fine. I'll give you that."

Somehow, Kat didn't see that tidbit doing

much to whittle down their pool of suspects. Even if Landon had limited his advances to the female population, he very well could have left some irate male partners in his path.

Frieda plucked a few of Tom's hairs from her blouse. "I should mention, these past few months he'd started acting rather funny."

Her change in demeanor prompted Kat to stand up straighter. Was Landon's widow finally going to reveal something useful?

But when Frieda didn't say anything more after a full ten seconds had passed, Kat realized she would have to draw the information out of her. "Funny how?" she asked.

"Secretive, I guess you'd say. Recently, like in the past year, he had taken to checking the mail."

"The mail?" That didn't sound like the promising lead Kat had hoped for.

Frieda lifted her eyes up. "I've always been the one to bring in the mail. But lately Landon had started grabbing it before I got home from work."

"Maybe he was trying to do more around the house," Marigold proposed, but her voice was weak, as though even she didn't believe it.

"My first thought was that he had a pen pal," Frieda said.

"You mean someone he was exchanging love letters with?" Kat asked.

Frieda nodded miserably.

"That's rather old-fashioned, isn't it?" Marigold put in.

Frieda shrugged. "It also leaves less of a trail than texting or emailing."

She had a point there. "You never saw any of these letters?" Kat asked.

"No."

"Did you ever witness Landon writing to this person?"

Frieda shook her head. "I checked his computer once, in case he typed out his replies, but there was nothing. And I'm pretty sure he destroyed whatever she sent him right after he read it. I spied him in the den shredding an envelope once, a couple months ago. When he noticed me, he jumped like I had poured water over his head. That's when I first started thinking there might be something off about him bringing in the mail."

Kat's heart sank. Without a trail leading back to Landon's mail buddy, it was unlikely they would ever find out who it was.

"Do you have any reason to believe this person might have been at Chief Kenny's party?" Kat asked.

Frieda wrinkled her brow. "No, I don't suppose so."

"Unless she's somebody from high school," Marigold interjected. "Could be she and Kenny are friends now, and he invited her to Imogene's."

Kat thought back to her breakfast with the Bridges. Landon's only ties to Cherry Hills seemed to be the ones he'd formed during his high school days.

Now she just had to figure out who from his past would still resent the man enough to want him dead thirty-some-odd years later.

CHAPTER EIGHT

"Kat, you're here," Imogene Little said. She waved Kat inside her house with both hands.

Kat stepped into the foyer. "I told you I'd be right over. You sounded pretty insistent on the phone."

Imogene slammed the door shut but didn't move into the living area. Instead, she stood there, wringing her hands together. "Yes, well, I was curious whether you've made any headway on this murder business."

"Shouldn't you be asking Chief Kenny that? Or Andrew?" *Or Raoul Leon,* Kat thought, although she still felt a spark of doubt when she recalled the way he'd gone about her witness interview.

"I just hate to bother them." Imogene sagged against the foyer wall, her imploring eyes boring into Kat's. "And I was under the impression Marigold had gotten in touch with you—to request your assistance in clearing her and Frieda."

Kat gaped at her. "How did you know that?" She had only left Frieda's hotel room an hour ago.

"I have my sources."

Sometimes Kat forgot how well connected Imogene was in Cherry Hills. Although, in this case, she suspected her friend's 'source' was the police chief himself.

Clover trotted into view. He paused in the middle of the living room, craning his neck to peer at them in the foyer. When he spotted Imogene, he let out a trill, his fluffy white tail sweeping back and forth.

"Yes, yes, I know, Clover," Imogene told him with a sigh.

"Is it his lunchtime?" Kat guessed.

"No, he's telling me he's disgusted by how I've been moping around and I need to buck up and get on with things."

Kat didn't see how Imogene had gathered all that from one tiny chirrup, but she wasn't in any position to question the communication methods between pets and their humans. She often carried on whole conversations with Matty and Tom, although usually only Tom could be bothered to reply.

Imogene's eyes drifted to her home office. "We usually spend Sunday mornings in there together, Clover curled up in his armchair and me attending to business."

Kat saw that the office door was still closed, and an ache bloomed in her chest. Imogene was no stranger to violent crime after several unfortunate incidences had occurred around town in the past year, but having her home serve as the scene of the offense had clearly gotten to her.

"The thought of going anywhere near that room gives me the heebie-jeebies," Imogene said. "Can you imagine? Afraid to enter my own office—my sanctuary!" She shook her head in disgust. "It's an abomination."

"Your feelings are only natural," Kat told her gently. "A man did die in there, after all."

Clover jumped onto the coffee table and glowered at Kat. Evidently the feline didn't appreciate his human being coddled.

Kat's eyes snagged on the sheet of paper poking out from beneath Clover's hind paws. A familiar smiling fruit basket peeked at her from the top left corner of the page. It was the

Easton's Eats invoice Kat had passed on to
Imogene before Imogene had left her apartment
late last night.

Imogene heaved a sigh as she followed the
direction of Kat's gaze. "I know I should pay
Sam for the wonderful job he did catering
Kenny's bash, but with my checkbook in my
desk, and my desk being in my office . . ."

"I understand," Kat said.

Clover hopped off the coffee table and
stomped over to the closed office door. He
planted his butt on the floor and looked at
Imogene with icy blue eyes.

Imogene bit her lip. "I don't know, Clover.
Just the thought of *peeking* in there makes my
stomach turn."

Clover twisted around to stare at the door,
his tail beating against the floor. He was
obviously a proponent of tough love.

"You know what, you're right." Imogene
squared her shoulders. "Enough excuses. I can't
put my life on hold forever, and Sam has a
business to run. It's not his fault Landon died.
Why should he have to wait to get paid because
of that?"

Her head held high, Imogene snatched up
Sam Easton's invoice and marched resolutely
through the living room. She stopped to pat

Clover on the head, then reached for the doorknob. He beat her into the room, squeezing
through the opening as soon as it was wide
enough to accommodate his body.

"Is there anything I can do to help?" Kat
asked, following behind them.

Imogene dropped into the chair behind her
desk, grabbed a pen, and clicked the ballpoint
out. "Just your presence here is a help."

Clover started sniffing the carpet. Kat's
stomach lurched when she saw the stain that
had captured his attention. Was that Landon's
blood? No wonder Imogene hadn't wanted to
come in here.

"Kenny promised me he would see to getting
that cleaned up," Imogene said.

Kat tore her eyes away from the carpet and
looked at her friend. She still had her pen in
hand, her head trained resolutely forward.

"I saw you shudder," Imogene explained.
"Don't worry, I had the same reaction."

"Right." Kat sucked air into her lungs and
sat down in one of the room's armchairs,
reveling in the solid feel of it beneath her.

"Supposedly Kenny knows somebody who
can wash that right out." Imogene sniffed. "Of
course, that's not going to do me much good if
he keeps dragging his feet."

"Landon only died yesterday. I'm sure Chief Kenny has been busy trying to figure out who could have killed him."

"He's removed himself from the case, remember?"

Although Chief Kenny might not be officially investigating Landon's death, after her talk with Marigold Kat was fairly certain he didn't intend to stay out of it in the slightest. With both of his sisters as suspects, how could he not do a little snooping on his own?

Imogene dropped her pen onto the desk and clutched her temples. "I don't know why I care about getting that cleaned up anyway. I'd be much better off having this carpet torn out and new one installed. Even the most skilled cleaner won't be able to remove the . . . the . . ."

"Blood?" Kat ventured.

"*Taint*," Imogene corrected with a shiver.

As if sensing Imogene's need for comfort, Clover leaped onto the desk and padded over to her. He stretched out his neck to rub the top of his head against her chin.

Imogene hugged the cat to her chest. "I apologize for being such a downer. I don't know what's come over me."

"It's only natural to feel out of sorts after something like this."

"I had hoped Landon's killer would have been identified by now."

Imogene peered at Kat, as though to give her a chance to confess she did indeed know who had murdered Landon Tabernathy. When Kat didn't respond after an awkward moment, Imogene's shoulders slumped. Her dejection was enough to spur Clover into action. He began pacing across the desk, making sure to head-bump Imogene each time he passed her. Kat wondered if he felt guilty for demanding that she come in here.

In his vigor, his hind foot kicked the Easton's Eats invoice off the desk.

Imogene rubbed the scruff of Clover's neck, chuckling as she watched the page float toward the floor. "This is why I have a paperweight."

Kat surveyed Imogene's desk. "Where is your paperweight anyway?"

Imogene stopped petting Clover to look around. After a moment, she frowned. "That's bizarre. It should be here somewhere. Clover, did you move it?"

Imogene bent down to search around the base of her desk, but Kat wasn't hopeful she would find what she was looking for. She was recalling what Marigold had told her about Landon receiving a blow to the head. Type of object used: unknown.

Except, Kat thought with a chill, now she had a pretty good idea what the object had been.

CHAPTER NINE

"Afternoon, Kat," Sam Easton said, holding the glass door open.

"Hey." Kat inhaled the delicious aroma of grease and sugar as she entered the small shop. "I never knew you had a bakery here."

Sam closed the door. "Yeah, well, catering alone doesn't pay the bills."

"You don't look like you're open," she commented, noting how the only lights turned on were coming from the back.

"I'm never open."

Kat's surprise must have shown on her face. Sam laughed as he led her toward the rear of the shop.

"Everything baked here is shipped else-where for sale," he informed her. "Or used on catering jobs, obviously. I supply a few different restaurants and delis around town with pastries and desserts."

"Oh, I didn't realize."

"It's the only way I can afford to keep a commercial kitchen open."

The kitchen in question was breathtaking. With two long, metal counters stretching down the middle and mixers and convection ovens lining opposite sides of the room, the place looked efficient and modern.

Sam stood by the end of one counter. "I could probably do a decent business if I ever decided to open up the front, but that would mean hiring more staff and establishing regular hours. This way, I'm open on my own terms. It suits my temperament better."

"Whatever works for you," Kat said, smiling.

He straightened. "So, Imogene said she was sending you to deliver me a check?"

"Yes." Kat fished it out of her jeans pocket. "She's sorry she didn't pay you last night, when the party dispersed."

"No worries." Sam took the check from her. He gave it a cursory scan before tucking it into his breast pocket. "I'm sure she would have paid me if I had stuck around. But after what happened . . ."

"Right." Kat experienced an unwelcome bout of dizziness as an image of Imogene's blood-stained carpet popped into her head.

"Whoa." Sam grabbed her arm. "You okay?"

Kat drew in a breath, managing to bob her head.

"Here, sit down." He guided her over to a waist-high canister of flour, plopping her onto the lid. "Rest here for a moment while I write out Imogene's receipt."

"Okay."

Sam walked down the aisle between the two counters. When he reached the end, a short young man with close-cropped black hair emerged from a nearby walk-in cooler, a box of apples in his hands. He carried the full box effortlessly, although his muscles bulged underneath his thin, black T-shirt.

"Rich," Sam said, stopping to greet the young man. "Still working on the apple tarts, I see."

"The first batch is in the oven," Rich replied, setting the box on the counter.

"Good, good. I'll be out to help in a minute."

"Sure thing, boss."

Sam gave him a nod before disappearing through a doorway on the far side of the room. Kat could see a desk and filing cabinets inside.

Rich started in Kat's direction, but he came to a dead halt when he spotted her.

She smiled at him. "Hi. I'm Kat."

Rich looked around as if something in the kitchen might explain her presence.

"I'm just waiting for Sam," she told him.

He aimed a finger in her direction. "I need to get some flour."

"Oh." Kat scrambled off her perch, grateful that her dizzy spell had passed.

Rich flipped the lid to the flour container open. Although he didn't make eye contact, Kat could tell he was still watching her as he reached for one of the glass measuring cups lined up along the back of the counter and dipped it into the flour.

Kat observed his movements, trying to work out why his name sounded familiar. Then it clicked. While she was waiting to be interviewed by Raoul, Sam Easton had mentioned a Rich had called in sick right before Imogene's party. Except, with his rosy cheeks and bright eyes, this Rich certainly didn't look sick.

"How are you feeling?" she asked.

Rich's head jerked up, a bemused slant to his lips. "Okay, I guess."

"Sam mentioned you were under the weather. He said you called in sick yesterday."

"Oh." Rich flushed crimson. He turned his back to her and dragged an industrial-sized mixing bowl closer. "Yeah, I wasn't feeling well. But I'm okay now."

Kat studied him as he dumped the contents of the measuring cup into the bowl. His movements were jerky, and flour sprayed everywhere, coating the counter with a circle of white dust. It was clear he was nervous about something, but what? Had he called in sick simply because he hadn't wanted to spend his Saturday working? Maybe Sam had yet to notice his curious overnight recovery, and he was worried she'd say something to him.

Rich paused to glance at her as he bent down to refill his measuring cup. She must have looked as suspicious as she felt because he quickly averted his eyes again.

"It must have been one of those twenty-four-hour things," he said. "Or maybe allergies."

"Or," Kat said, measuring her words, "maybe you weren't really sick at all."

His hand froze inside the flour container.

Kat took a step closer and lowered her voice to a conspiratorial whisper. "Sam's going to be back any minute now. I don't want him to overhear us if it will get you in trouble, so if you want to come clean, now's your chance to do so without having to answer to your boss."

A muscle in Rich's jaw twitched as he appeared to mull over her words. Then he released a long, slow breath, straightening away from the flour container.

"Okay, here's the deal," he said, his eyes darting toward the doorway where Sam had disappeared. "I wasn't really sick. Deirdre called me up yesterday morning and asked if I'd let her work my shift."

Kat conjured up an image of the brunette server. "Did she say why?"

"She needed the money. And I'm doing okay right now, so I figured why not help her out a little."

"Why didn't you just explain that to Sam?"

"Because he wouldn't have agreed to switch us out. Working the party put Deirdre on overtime. He hates that."

Kat nodded. Limiting overtime hours seemed like a valid goal for a small business owner.

"Don't tell Sam, okay?" Rich whispered. "I don't want him thinking I'm the type of guy who calls in sick when he's not. This is a good job. I don't want to lose it."

Kat made a motion of zipping her lips. "Your

secret's safe with me."

Rich looked relieved, offering her a soft smile.

"Here we are!" Sam called out.

The tension that had drained from Rich's posture returned just as quickly. He twisted away from Kat, busying himself with measuring out more flour.

Sam waved a sheet of paper in front of Kat. "Here's Imogene's receipt, fresh off the printer."

Kat took it from him. "Thanks."

He headed toward the front. "I'll show you out."

Kat waited until they were at the door before she said, "I was wondering if you could help me reach one of your caterers."

Sam paused with his hand on the door's bar handle. "One of my caterers?"

"The brunette woman who was working Chief Kenny's birthday party."

"You mean Deirdre Solomon?"

Kat felt a frisson of electricity shoot through her. "Solomon?"

Sam looked at her funny. "Yeah."

She thought back to Belinda and Colin's exchange at Jessie's Diner. Hadn't they mentioned a Rita Solomon attending high school with them way back when? Was there a chance Deirdre was related to Rita?

"Do you know how I can reach her?" she asked Sam.

"I do." He paused. "But, Kat, I'm not quite sure what you want with her. You don't think she had anything to do with what happened to Chief Kenny's brother-in-law, do you?"

"I'm not sure at this point," Kat hedged, not wanting to reveal too much. "But with her circling through the crowd, she likely saw more than most of the guests. I was hoping maybe she noticed someone slipping inside Imogene's office."

"Wouldn't she have told the police?"

"Maybe not." Kat thought fast. "She seemed so distraught yesterday I doubt she could think straight. And Officer Leon can be a little intimidating. She might have been afraid to admit to anything for fear he would hold her there longer."

Sam rubbed his chin. "You have a point there. Well, if you think it will help, Deirdre lives on Bermuda Avenue, in the apartment complex near the library. Just look for the unit with the green curtains."

Kat grinned. "Thank you."

She tried not to hurry as she exited the shop. Still, by the time she reached her car her

heart was racing so fast she felt as though she'd
run a marathon.

CHAPTER TEN

Deirdre Solomon lived in a drab apartment building sorely in need of renovation. When Deirdre opened her door, Kat could hear the hinges creaking.

"Oh, hello." Deirdre kept one hand on the doorknob, a look of uncertainty on her face. "Are you at the right place?"

"I am." Kat inched her foot forward, just in case Deirdre tried to slam the door in her face. "I'd like to talk to you about Imogene's party yesterday."

Deirdre tucked her hands inside her long-sleeved shirt, like a turtle retreating into its shell. "What about it?"

"I have reason to believe you might know who killed Landon Tabernathy," Kat said, watching Deirdre's reaction carefully.

Deirdre scooted partway behind the door as if she might be able to hide there. "Why would I know anything?"

Kat shrugged, then took a step forward, treating Deirdre's retreat as an invitation to enter. "Mind if we talk about this inside?"

Deirdre hesitated.

"Or I could ask Officer Leon to pay you an official visit," Kat said.

The threat had the desired effect. Deirdre held the door open wider.

The living area was small and cramped, making Kat feel a little claustrophobic as she and Deirdre sat across from each other on mismatched armchairs.

"Did you know Landon?" Kat asked.

"No," Deirdre said.

"Your mother did though, right?"

Deirdre stilled. When she spoke, her voice came out high and squeaky. "My mother?"

Kat nodded. "Your mother is Rita Solomon, right?"

Deirdre didn't respond. She merely stared at Kat with those huge, brown eyes.

"I heard she and Landon both attended Cherry Hills High at the same time. That must have been around, oh . . ." Kat tapped her chin, pretending to do the mental math. ". . . around thirty-two years ago."

"I—I guess that's about right."

Kat scrutinized Deirdre. "How old are you again?"

Deirdre squeezed her lips together until they turned white from the pressure.

"Deirdre," Kat said softly, "was Landon your father?"

Deirdre looked down at her lap, picking imaginary lint off of her slacks. Then, finally, she offered up a tiny nod.

"Was your mother at the party yesterday?" Kat asked.

"Ma?" Deirdre looked surprised by the question. "No."

Kat held her gaze. "Then it was you."

Deirdre didn't ask what she meant. It was clear she understood perfectly. The guilt was etched all over her face.

"I didn't want anything from him," she said, sounding like a lost little girl instead of a woman Kat's age. "I just wanted to get to know him."

"But he didn't care to know you," Kat guessed.

Deirdre's face darkened. "Except for one time, he couldn't even be bothered to write back when I sent him those letters."

So Landon's long-lost daughter had been his mystery pen pal rather than an illicit lover, Kat mused. Even so, she doubted Frieda would find any comfort in that fact.

"Ma said he was heartless, but I guess a part of me never truly believed her," Deirdre continued. "She wouldn't even tell me his name until I turned thirty. I guess she finally decided I had a right to know, even if she figured he would end up hurting me."

"Your mother didn't tell him when she found out she was pregnant with you?" Kat asked.

"She said she did."

"What did he do when she told him?"

"Nothing." Deirdre's look was hard. "He turned his back and walked away from her."

Kat hadn't known Landon, nor did she condone how he'd died, but she couldn't prevent the flash of anger that seared through her then on Rita Solomon's behalf.

"Ma left Cherry Hills soon after that," Deirdre said. "My grandparents, her parents, were old school, at least that's how Ma described them. They whisked her away from here as soon as they found out she was pregnant and told her not to tell anyone. She said they urged her to give me up for adoption. When she told them she planned to keep me, they disowned her. I never did meet them."

Kat's throat tightened. "So she was on her own. A high school senior with a baby to support by herself."

"She dropped out a month before graduation. She had to juggle two jobs just to pay the rent, and she told me she worked right up until she went into labor. She didn't have time to keep up with her schoolwork. Heck, she barely had time for me. I hardly ever saw her when I was a kid. She was always leaving me with one of the neighbors. She had to. She couldn't afford day care."

"She didn't ask Landon for child support?"

Deirdre shrugged. "I never asked, but knowing Ma she wouldn't have pushed the issue. Despite her circumstances, she was proud. Too proud. She viewed asking for help as a weakness."

Kat nodded. "She was independent."

"To a fault. If Ma had made Landon step up back when she first found out she was going to have me, maybe he would have married her instead of that other woman. Ma never would have had to drop out of school. She'd be a surgeon earning millions instead of a sales clerk making peanuts."

Deirdre had obviously convinced herself that all her problems would have been solved if only her father had been around. Kat didn't deny her her delusions. After all, who was she to say how things would have worked out if Rita Solomon's pregnancy had come to light before Landon had proposed to Frieda? It was impossible to know where the path not taken might have led.

Deirdre's eyes filled with tears. "I was so sure he would want to get to know me. But when I started reaching out to him on social media, he blocked me. I figured maybe he thought I was a troll or something. So I tracked down his home address and sent him a letter asking if we could talk."

"But he didn't respond?" Kat asked.

"Oh, no, he responded that first time." Deirdre's nostrils flared. "That was the one and only time I got a reply back."

"What did he say?"

"That he already had a family, that him and his wife were happy, that they'd never wanted children, and he had no use for one now." She sniffled. "How could he not want to know his own flesh and blood?"

Kat could just imagine how small and

inconsequential Deirdre must have felt when she'd read that letter from Landon. What kind of person could reject their own child? One who never wanted to be a parent in the first place, she supposed.

For that matter, how had Rita Solomon felt when her own parents tossed her aside just when she'd needed them the most? She must have been so lonely and terrified.

Deirdre swiped at her tears with one shirt-sleeve. "Anyway, I wasn't going to let him off that easily. Ma might have been okay with him ignoring me, but I wasn't. So I kept writing him. He could block me online, but he couldn't stop my letters from being delivered to his house. Even if he didn't read them, just seeing my name on that envelope would be a reminder that I existed whether he liked it or not."

"And he never replied after that first time?"

"Nope. Never."

"Then how did you know he would be at that party yesterday?" Kat asked.

"Imogene called Sam in the morning to go over the details. I was in the kitchen prepping some of the food, and Sam had her on speaker-phone in his office. She was excited about Chief Kenny's sisters driving over here for his birthday. She mentioned Landon and his wife by name. It was like kismet. For the first time since I'd found out who he was, my father was returning to Cherry Hills."

"So you asked Rich if you could work his shift," Kat said.

Deirdre nodded. "I made up a story about being short on next month's rent, and he was nice enough to agree to call in sick and let me fill in for him."

"And what was your plan? What did you hope to accomplish by seeing Landon at the party? He had already made it clear he didn't want to talk to you."

"I thought maybe if he met me in person he would change his mind." Deirdre's face fell. "But when I went up to him and told him who I was, he got mad."

Kat's heart skipped a beat. "Did he try to hurt you?"

"No, but he shooed me away, like I was some kind of pest, a fly or a gnat." Her jaw grew taut. "I told him I wasn't going anywhere, that he owed me a conversation at the very least."

Kat could see the pain in Deirdre's eyes as she replayed Landon's rejection in her head, and her heart ached for her. She couldn't help it. Despite how the woman sitting across from her might technically be a murderer, it was clear she was also simply a lost girl who longed for her father. Kat could sympathize. She had also grown up without a father.

Deirdre drew in a deep breath. "He must have realized I wasn't going anywhere because he said fine, that he'd talk to me, but not where anyone could hear us. He grabbed my arm and dragged me into Imogene's office."

"Then what happened?" Kat asked.

"Then he asked what I wanted, gruffly, like I was inconveniencing him. But I thought this might be the only chance I had, so I told him I wanted to get to know him, that I didn't have much family, since Ma's side had disowned her."

"How did he respond to that?"

"He didn't care. I don't think he was even really listening to me. He kept glancing at the door, like he couldn't wait to get back to the party." Deirdre's hands clenched into fists. "And then he had the nerve to turn his back on me."

"And that made you angry," Kat filled in.

"Of course it made me angry. Wouldn't you be angry if your father wouldn't even grant you the courtesy of a single conversation?"

Kat swallowed. "Is that why you killed him?"

"That's when I threw the paperweight at him. I didn't really think, I just saw it sitting there so I picked it up and hurled it in his direction."

Deirdre stared off into space, her eyes unfocused. Watching her, Kat's chest felt too tight.

"He made a sound when it hit him, like an *oomph*. Then he fell to the ground and didn't move." Deirdre rubbed her fists in her eye sockets. "There was blood. I didn't expect that. I didn't mean to kill him. I only wanted to get his attention, to get him to *see* me."

Kat sagged against the chair. Deirdre might not have meant to kill Landon, but that didn't change the fact that she had—or the fact that she'd left him for dead. And no matter how badly Landon had hurt her, it would be insufficient justification for taking his life in any court of law.

"Where is the paperweight now?" Kat asked.

Deirdre's hands fell back into her lap. Then she pointed to the kitchen. "In the garbage pail under the sink. I didn't want to leave it at the party, with my fingerprints on it. But now I guess it doesn't really matter." Her eyes searched Kat's face. "I'm going to prison, aren't I?"

Kat didn't have the heart to answer. But she didn't think Deirdre was really looking for an answer either. She already knew how this story ended, the same way it had begun, with one man forever altering the course of a young girl's life when he chose to walk away without a single backward glance.

CHAPTER ELEVEN

❝On behalf of the entire Cherry Hills Police Department, I'd like to thank you for your help in solving Landon's murder," Chief Kenny said, grabbing hold of Kat's right hand and pumping it heartily between his own as he dragged her inside Imogene's house.

"Oh." Kat extracted her hand from his grasp before he crushed it. "I'm sure Andrew and Raoul would have solved it if I hadn't."

"Oh, now, I don't know about that," Imogene piped up from where she sat on one of her living room sofas. "Raoul Leon's so green you could toss him in a salad."

Chief Kenny chuckled as he planted himself beside Imogene. "You would know, eating like a bunny."

Imogene slapped him playfully on the shoulder.

Kat sat down in a nearby armchair. "I hope Raoul's not too disappointed that he wasn't the one to break the case." She also hoped he wasn't too upset that she'd phoned Andrew instead of him after Deirdre had confessed. Although she didn't really care for Raoul, she still felt a little guilty for once thinking he might have had a hand in Landon's death.

Chief Kenny stroked Clover when the white cat jumped onto his lap. "Don't you worry your pretty little head about Raoul. He's still got plenty of detective work to keep him busy."

Alarm flitted across Imogene's face. "Has there been another murder?"

"No, sirree." Chief Kenny grinned. "Raoul's learning how real detectives fill their days—with good ol'-fashioned paperwork."

"Are you going to promote him permanently?" Kat asked.

"I reckon one of these days I'll do just that. But I ain't got the budget for it yet."

Imogene crossed her ankles. "Well, now that this case is solved, you can focus on getting my office cleaned."

"That's next on my list, right after I file my own paperwork," he replied.

"Oh, Kenny." Imogene frowned at him. "How long is that going to take?"

"Not more than a day or two."

Clover gave the police chief a dirty look. Apparently Imogene wasn't the only human he preferred to handle with tough love.

Imogene flashed Chief Kenny a dirty look of her own. "You have one day. Then I'm taking matters into my own hands and sending you the bill."

"Aw, now, don't pout. I said I'd take care of it, and I'm a man of my word."

"What's taking so long anyway?"

"I've been shopping around, looking for the same shade of carpet you've got here. They don't make this kind anymore."

Imogene's lips curved up. "You mean you're having the carpet replaced, not just cleaned?"

"Yep. Figured you could sleep easier that way."

"Well . . . thank you. I appreciate it."

"You're very welcome." Chief Kenny reached into his breast pocket. "Here, I've got a little something else for you, too."

Imogene sucked in a breath when she saw what was in his hand. Kat scooted forward, trying to get a better look herself. Her heart stopped beating when she spied the velvet-covered box.

"Now don't go making a big fuss," Chief Kenny said, a bead of sweat materializing on his forehead. "It's nothing fancy, just something that caught my eye when I was out looking at carpet."

Imogene didn't seem to hear him. She snatched the box from his hands and popped the lid off. Kat couldn't see what was inside, but from the way Imogene's smile slipped, she didn't figure it was an engagement ring.

"It's a paperweight," Chief Kenny said. He ruffled Clover's fur. "Looks like the spitting image of this little guy, huh? Thought you might like it after what happened with your other."

Imogene reached into the box and lifted up a white, ceramic cat. Kat could see now the box was much too large to hold a ring.

Clover scrambled to his feet and hissed at the offending creature. He took a swipe at it with one paw, knocking it to the floor.

"Clover!" Imogene scooped the paperweight off the carpet. "Behave yourself!"

"Hey now, buddy." Chief Kenny rubbed Clover between his ears. "Don't go getting your tail in a knot. It ain't real."

Clover clearly didn't appreciate the advice. He glared at the humans before hopping onto the floor and trotting over to Kat. He joined her on the armchair, where he laid down on her lap and subjected the others to a death stare.

Imogene didn't pay him any attention. Her smile was back in full force now as she gazed at Chief Kenny. "Thank you, Kenny. But you didn't have to buy me this."

He grinned, looking more relaxed in the face of Imogene's approval. "It was my pleasure."

"But I didn't even get you anything for your birthday."

"What're you clucking about? You threw me a party."

"A party with food you hated."

Chief Kenny grimaced. "This pains me to say, but that peahen wheelbarrow thingy wasn't half bad."

"You mean the chickpea pinwheel?" Imogene squinted at him. "You tried it?"

"What else could I do? The dang thing was falling apart in my hands."

Imogene hooted with pleasure, then hugged the paperweight to her chest. "I'm going to treasure this."

Clover's tail pummeled Kat's stomach. She petted him, hoping the surly feline wouldn't break the new paperweight at his first opportunity. It might very well be the first present

Chief Kenny had ever given Imogene.

Imogene rested her head on Chief Kenny's shoulder. "Okay, you're forgiven for the carpet—for now. Any more delays though and I'll be expecting more presents."

"Deal."

Watching them, Kat had to smile. If she'd had any lingering doubts about them being more than friends, the way they were snuggling together banished them. Whether or not Imogene and Chief Kenny chose to acknowledge their attraction in public, it was clear they shared more than a platonic connection.

She thought about Landon Tabernathy and Deirdre Solomon, two people who shared a genetic connection but not much else. She wondered if Deirdre had ever experienced the kind of love she had so desperately craved from her father. Kat hoped so, because one thing she had learned in her thirty-two years was that you didn't necessarily need genetics to tie you to someone.

Sometimes the best family wasn't the one you were born into, but the one you created for yourself.

NOTE FROM THE AUTHOR

Thank you for visiting Cherry Hills, home of Kat, Matty, and Tom! If you enjoyed their story, please consider leaving a book review on your favorite retailer and/or review site.

Keep reading for an excerpt from Book Nineteen of the Cozy Cat Caper Mystery series, *Arson in Cherry Hills*. Thank you!

Excerpt From

ARSON
in CHERRY
HILLS

PAIGE SLEUTH

" This is nice, huh?" Andrew Milhone said, squeezing Katherine Harper's hand as they strolled along the sidewalk.

"It sure is," Kat agreed. She breathed in the crisp, April air. Sunny but still early enough for there to be a slight chill, it was the perfect morning for a walk.

Although, she considered, they weren't walking so much as creeping at a snail's pace behind Matty. And the curious yellow-and-brown tortoiseshell had made it infinitely clear she wasn't in any hurry. Every two steps she found something interesting enough to stop and sniff, whether it be a sidewalk crack, a bush, or even a simple blade of grass.

"I'm glad you suggested this," Kat said,

watching as a bird alighted two yards away. The bird cocked its head and peered at Matty with one beady eye. Matty hunkered lower into the grass, her gray-striped tail cutting back and forth like a scythe. "We should do this more often."

Andrew unlaced his fingers from Kat's and ran his hand through his sandy hair, pushing back the piece that kept falling into his eyes. "Actually, there's something I wanted to tell you."

Kat stilled, his tone putting her on alert. "Oh?"

"I'm having dinner with somebody tonight."

The ground shifted beneath her. "Dinner?"

"Yeah. She texted me yesterday, asking if we could get together."

Alarm bells rang in Kat's head. *She?* Although they had never discussed it, Kat had been under the impression she and Andrew were dating exclusively. He had never mentioned an interest in seeing other people during their eight months together. In fact, they had both exchanged 'I love you's only a couple months ago. Could he be tired of her already?

Andrew grabbed her hand and gripped it tight. "Oh, no, it's not a date."

"Okay," Kat said, although her stomach was

still somewhere near her feet.

"She's my sister."

"Wait." Kat twisted to face him better. "Your sister is in Cherry Hills? You mean the half-sister you've never met and didn't even know existed until several years ago?"

Andrew nodded. "She emailed me yesterday asking if we could get together. She flew into Seattle to check out some master's program at U-Dub, and since we're only a couple hours east she figured she might as well spend the weekend here."

"Huh." Kat took a moment to process that. "What is she studying?"

"Psychology. Or maybe it was pharmacy." He pursed his lips. "Philosophy?"

Kat laughed, the last of her tension fading away. "So basically you have no clue."

"Hey, I was too focused on the fact I'd get to meet her."

"Is she staying at your house?"

"No, Alyssa—that's her name—booked a room at the Cherry Hills Hotel."

"Alyssa," Kat repeated, turning it over in her head.

Matty's nose twitched as the bird finally took off. The feline tracked its progress into the sky, then turned her attention to inspecting the bushes again.

Andrew kicked a stone on the sidewalk. "Her train to Wenatchee should have gotten in late last night, then she was going to cab it to Cherry Hills. Did I tell you she's from Boston? I guess people there are used to not driving anywhere. Anyway, she wanted to do lunch today, but I'm on duty until five. But I still want to keep this casual and not turn it into a big Saturday night affair. I was thinking of taking her to Jessie's. It's homey, relaxed, nothing unpronounceable on the menu. I don't want this to feel like a big deal."

"Not a big deal, right." Except, in Kat's opinion it was a very big deal. And judging by the uncharacteristic way Andrew was babbling on, he obviously thought it was a big deal, too.

That wasn't a surprise given their history. Kat and Andrew had both grown up in foster care until they'd graduated high school close to sixteen years ago now. At the time, neither one had any siblings they were aware of. But that didn't stop Kat from dreaming about a big sister to confide in, someone with whom she could share all her hopes and fears. Sometimes she'd wanted it so badly her yearning had left a physical ache in her gut.

And now Andrew was living her dream.

Well, maybe not exactly, but close enough that she couldn't help but feel a twinge of jealousy.

But this was about him, not her, she reminded herself.

"Well," she said, smiling at him, "I think that sounds nice, even if I was kind of hoping we could get together tonight."

She waited for Andrew to invite her to join them for dinner, but apparently her hint had been too subtle. "I'm meeting her right after I get off work," he said. "I figure we'll finish supper by eight at the latest. Then maybe you and I could hang out."

"You mean like a debriefing."

"I suppose you could call it that."

Matty had grown bored and was now inching farther down the sidewalk. Kat and Andrew fell into step behind her.

"Well, sure," Kat said. "I can do a debriefing. Besides, I'm curious to learn more about this mysterious sister of yours."

"Me, too."

Kat didn't miss the quaver in his voice. She set her leash-free hand on his arm and stood on her tiptoes to plant a kiss on his cheek. "She's going to love you."

He gazed into her eyes. "You think so?"

"I know so."

He grinned, twin dimples appearing on opposite sides of his mouth. He pressed his lips against hers, but the kiss only lasted a second before Kat felt the leash pull against her fingers.

She sighed and refocused her attention on Matty. The tortoiseshell had her nose tilted up, her whiskers twitching as though she smelled something. A bird or a dog was probably nearby, Kat figured.

She likely would have stuck with that assumption if she hadn't caught a whiff of something herself at that exact moment.

She wrinkled her nose. "Do you smell smoke?"

Alarm flashed in Andrew's eyes. "Something's burning over there."

Kat pivoted around, her heart lodging in her throat when she spied thick wisps of black ash rising into the air. It seemed to be coming from only a few blocks away—and it looked a lot more serious than a backyard barbecue gone wrong.

* * *

Please check your favorite online retailer for availability.

ABOUT THE AUTHOR

Paige Sleuth is a pseudonym for mystery author Marla Bradeen. She plots murder during the day and fights for mattress space with her two rescue cats at night. When not attending to her cats' demands, she writes. She loves to hear from readers, and welcomes emails at: paige.sleuth@yahoo.com

If you'd like to join Paige's readers' group, please visit: http://hyperurl.co/readersgroup

9 781978 373839

CPSIA informatio
at www.ICGtestin
Printed in the USA
LVOW03s080520
560362LV0